Text copyright © 2000 by Nicola Moon
Illustrations copyright © 2000 by Carol Thompson
All rights reserved.

CIP Data is available.

Published in the United States 2001 by Dutton Children's Books,
a division of Penguin Putnam Books for Young Readers
345 Hudson Street, New York, New York 10014
www.penguinputnam.com

Originally published in Great Britain 2000 by Orchard Books, London
Typography by Alan Carr · Printed in Dubai
First American Edition · ISBN 0-525-46780-7
2 4 6 8 10 9 7 5 3 1

My Most Favorite Thing

BY Nicola Moon · ILLUSTRATED BY Carol Thompson

DUTTON CHILDREN'S BOOKS · NEW YORK

Rabbit's tail

Rabbit

Rabbit's ear

For Imogen
N.M.

For Basil
C.T.

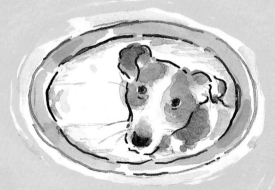

Billy

Katie had a stuffed bunny named Rabbit. He was very old and battered, with one and a half ears and no tail, but Katie loved him.

Everywhere Katie went, Rabbit went, too.
Rabbit shared everything.

Mealtime. Playtime. Bath time. And
especially hug time.

"Rabbit is my most favorite thing in all
the world," said Katie.

mealtime

playtime

bath time

hug time

Katie knew that Grandpa's most favorite thing in all the world was his dog, Billy. Billy had floppy ears, a funny, stumpy tail, and big brown eyes. Everywhere Grandpa went, Billy went, too.

Grandpa had a big jar in the
kitchen full of special doggy treats.
Katie liked to watch Billy wag
his stumpy tail and look up at
Grandpa with his big brown eyes,
until Grandpa just *had* to give him a treat.
In the evenings, Grandpa liked to watch
television with Billy curled
up on the sofa
beside him.

One Saturday, Katie and Rabbit went to Grandpa's house.

But Billy didn't jump up when he saw Katie. He didn't even wag his stumpy tail. He just looked up at her with sad brown eyes.

"What's wrong with him?" said Katie.

"Poor Billy isn't well," said Grandpa. "I think we'd better take him to the vet."

Katie hugged Rabbit very tightly while they sat in the vet's waiting room. Then it was their turn, and Grandpa took Billy in to see the vet.

When Grandpa came out, he was alone. "Billy has to stay here," he said. "There's something wrong in Billy's tummy, and he has to have an operation."

"Will it make Billy better?" Katie asked.

"I hope so," said Grandpa.

Grandpa's house felt empty without Billy.

"Will Billy be all right on his own at the vet's?"
Katie asked.

"Yes," said Grandpa. "There are other animals there and
kind people to look after him."

Katie knew that Grandpa and Billy were always together.
Billy was Grandpa's most favorite thing in all the world.
And now Billy was sick, and Grandpa was all alone.

When it was time for Katie to go home, she
picked up Rabbit and squeezed him tight.

Then she pushed him into Grandpa's hand.
"Rabbit wants to stay with you, Grandpa," she
said. "So you won't be lonely in the night."

Then Grandpa hugged Katie and hugged
Rabbit all at the same time.

That night in bed, Katie felt very strange without Rabbit.

She had Teddy instead. But Teddy didn't feel like Rabbit, and he didn't smell like Rabbit.

Rabbit was far away, tucked up in bed with Grandpa.

But Rabbit would look after Grandpa,
and Grandpa would look after Rabbit . . .
until Billy was better.

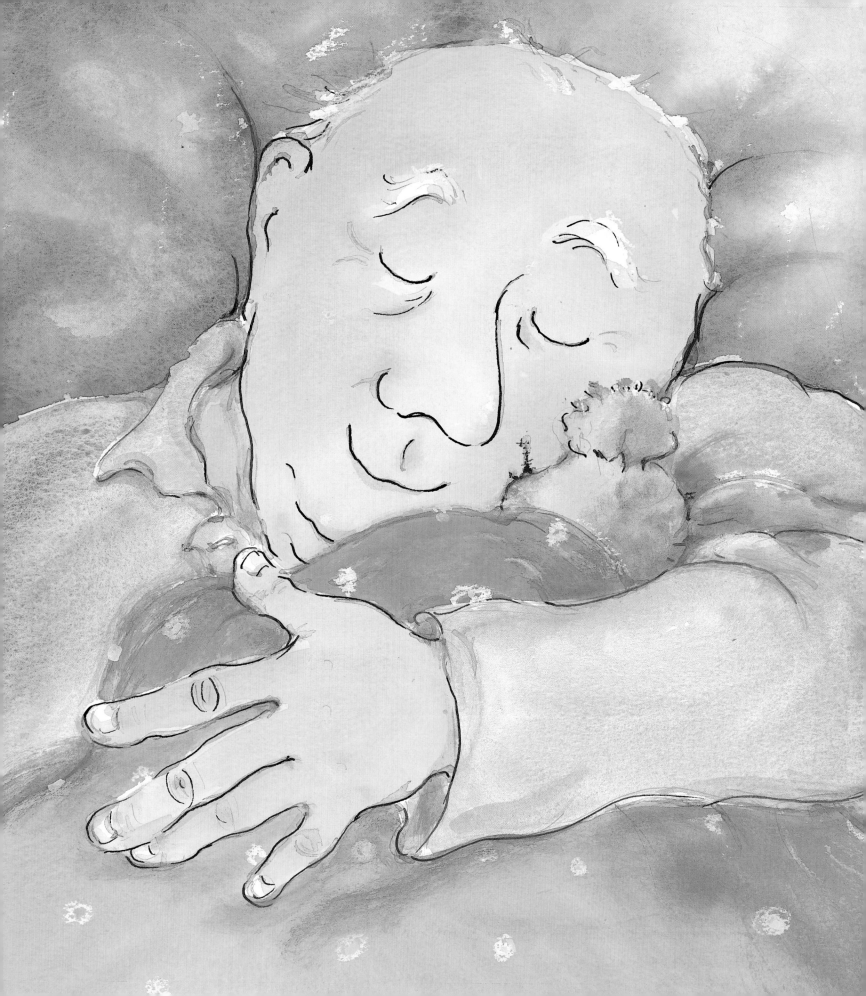

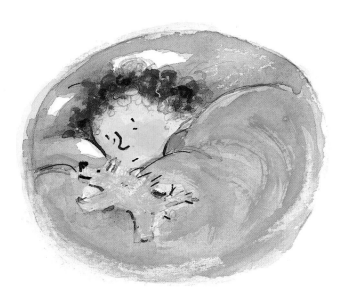

Rabbit stayed with Grandpa the next night, too.
This time, Katie took Fluffy Dog to bed with
her. But Fluffy Dog wasn't the right shape to
cuddle, and his fur made her nose itchy. It took
Katie a long time to go to sleep.

The next day, the phone rang.

"That was Grandpa," said Mom.

"It's Billy! Is Billy better?" asked Katie.

Billy *was* better!

They rushed to Grandpa's house. Katie gave Billy a big hug, and Billy wagged his funny, stumpy tail.

"Here's someone else to see you," said Grandpa.
"Rabbit wants to come home now."

Katie hugged Rabbit. "Rabbit is my most
favorite thing in all the world!" said Katie.
"And Billy's my most
favorite dog!"

"And here's my most favorite *person* in all the world," said Grandpa, picking up Katie and swinging her high in the air.

"And Rabbit," said Katie.

"And Rabbit, of course," said Grandpa.

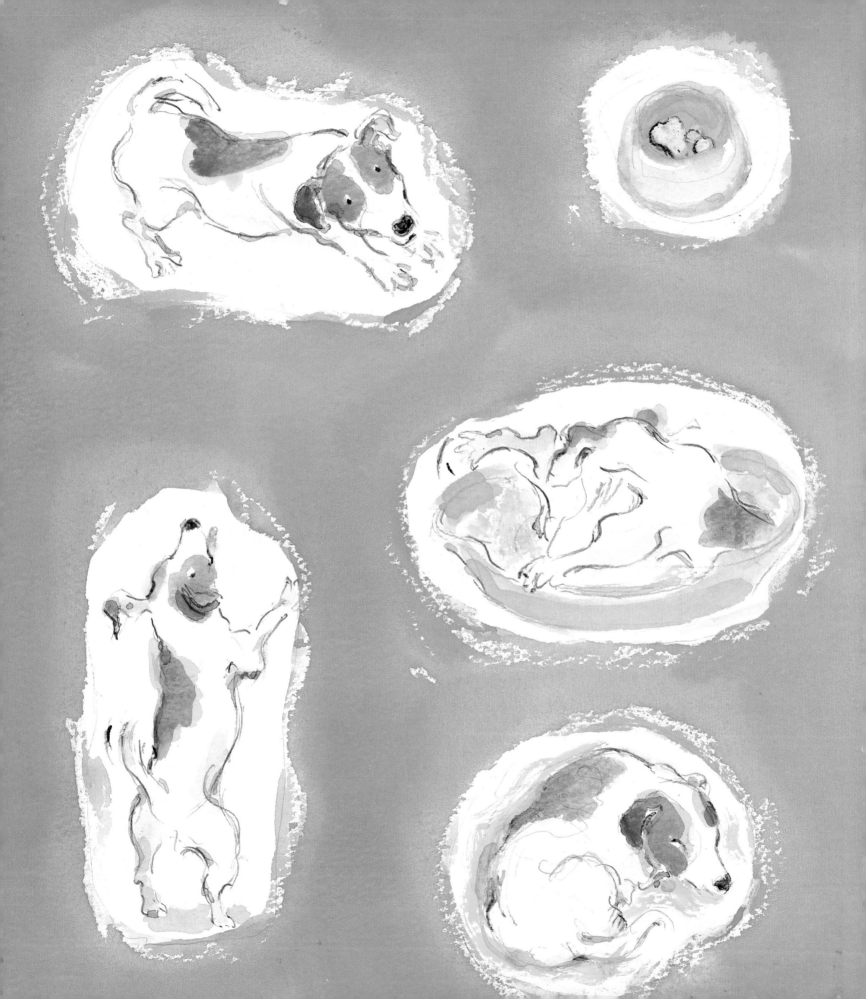